This Orchard book

belongs to

....

TEN LITTLE BUGS

MIKE BROWNLOW   SIMON RICKERTY

ORCHARD

Ten little jitterbugs prepare for Moonbeam Ball.
The Bug Hotel will host it, in their Creepy Crawly Hall.

The Queen Bee and the Emperor will both be coming too.

Ready Bugs? There's lots to do! The bugs all shout,

"WOO-HOO!"

Ten little jitterbugs

need party lights to shine.

10

. . . nine.

Nine little jitterbugs – what
will the wasps create?

9

OooOOOOoo!

Lots of party costumes! Thanks!

Now there are . . .

. . . eight.

Eight little jitterbugs cry,

"Party's at eleven . . .

HEY! Butterflies! We hope you'll come!"

8

Now there are . . .

. . . seven.

Seven little jitterbugs with boxes, string and sticks.

BISH!

7

BASH!

BANG!

"Let's make the stage!"

Now there are . . .

. . . six.

Six little jitterbugs,
invited to the hive.

6

. . . five.

Five little jitterbugs are busy
with their chores, when . . .

CHOMP!

goes the caterpillar!

Now there are . . .

. . . four.

Four little jitterbugs –

the ants march perfectly.

STOMP!

4

STOMP! STOMP!

Yum, party food! Now there are . . .

. . . three.

Three little jitterbugs

collect the evening dew.

3

PLINK!

The perfect party drink!

Now there are . . .

. . . two.

Two little jitterbugs –
the spider's web is spun.

BOING!

A bouncy game to play!

Now there's

only . . .

. . . **one.**

One little jitterbug
puzzles what to do.

Who will play the music?
Hmm? They must be good,
but who?

1

Ah-ha!

The Bugs are all assembled and
the dancing's still to come.

But who will be the stars tonight?
They hear a guitar strum . . .

"We have a treat for everyone – the best band anywhere!

So Bugs – please welcome to the stage . . .
THE BEETLES!! Yeah! Yeah! Yeah!"

"The Ball's a triumph," says the queen.

"Our thanks to all of you!"

For Rowan, (who loves bugs!) – M.B.

For Hilary - my wonderful agent. Thank you for your amazing support, passion and dedication. x – S.R.

ORCHARD BOOKS

First published in Great Britain in 2023 by Orchard Books

1 3 5 7 9 10 8 6 4 2

Text © Mike Brownlow, 2023
Illustrations © Simon Rickerty, 2023

A CIP catalogue record for this book is available from the British Library.

ISBN 978 1 40836 665 3

Printed and bound in China

Orchard Books
An imprint of Hachette Children's Group
Part of Hodder & Stoughton Limited
Carmelite House
50 Victoria Embankment
London EC4Y 0DZ

An Hachette UK Company
www.hachette.co.uk

www.hachettechildrens.co.uk